D0461622

Tutus

Aren't

by Linda Skeers

Style

My

pictures by Anne Wilsdorf

Dial Books for Young Readers
an imprint of Penguin Group (USA) Inc.

Emma spent the morning catching frogs, roping the cat, and digging for pirate treasure.

Then the mailman said, "This is for you." And the day got even better!

Emma ripped open the package from Uncle Leo. She
was hoping for a pirate hat or a lizard.
The box was full of pink. No pirate hat.
It was soft and silky. No lizard.

Emma pulled out . . . a ballerina outfit.

What was Uncle Leo thinking?

Emma had never wanted to be a ballerina. But she didn't want to disappoint Uncle Leo. Especially since he was coming for a visit.

"I don't know *how* to be a ballerina," she said.

The mailman grinned. "You float like a fairy," he said, leaping across the lawn. "You flutter like a butterfly." He twirled and whirled. "And you dance like daisies and dandelion fluff!"

Emma floated.
And landed in the petunia patch.

She fluttered.
And tripped over the garden gnome.

She twirled.
And fell into the birdbath.

"I think you twirled when you should have whirled," said the mailman.
"What's so great about floating like fluff?" Emma mumbled.
She sat and looked at the ballerina outfit. She held up the satiny pink
slippers with long dangling ribbons.

Mrs. Gurkin was walking her poodles. "Oh, Emma!"
she said. "You'll make a lovely ballerina!"
"But I don't know *how*!" Emma said.

"With elegance and grace," Mrs. Gurkin replied. "And on your tippy-toes!" She took a handful of doggy treats from her pocket and held them high. Rufus and Lulu shimmied forward and boogied backward on their little puppy toes.

"Looks easy," said Emma. She slipped off her cowboy boots
and put on her slippers. She tied the ribbons in dainty little bows
around her ankles.

She stood on her right toe
and flopped over to the left.
It wasn't graceful.

She stood on her left toe
and toppled over to the right.
It wasn't elegant.

She stood on both toes and
fell backward. Into the petunia
patch. Again.

"Tippy-toes aren't my style," she muttered.

"Maybe you'd do better indoors," suggested Mrs. Gurkin.

Emma took the package into the house. If she put the whole outfit on, she might feel like a ballerina.

She slipped into the leotard. The tutu. The sparkly crown.

"*I still* don't know how to be a ballerina," Emma muttered.

Her big brother, Tony, strolled into the room. "If you want to be a ballerina, you need music," he said. "Flippy-fluttery music with violins, harps, and flutes."

"Music?" said Emma. "Yes! That's what I need!"

Emma didn't have a violin, harp, or flute. But she did have a kazoo. She played a little tune.

"How's that?" she asked.

"Sounds like burping," said Tony. "I don't think ballerinas are allowed to burp."

Emma plopped onto the floor. Being a ballerina was hard and everyone knew the rules.

Or did they?

The mailman said to float and flutter. Mrs. Gurkin said ballerinas dance on their tippy-toes. Tony said they need fancy music.

"Sounds like everyone has different rules about ballerinas," said Emma. "I'll make up my *own*!"

She somersaulted across the floor. "Ballerinas roll like tumbleweeds in a dust storm!"

She pulled on her cowboy boots. "And toes are meant for tapping!"

Slipping off the tutu, Emma put on her shorts. Now she had room for all her important stuff.

"And ballerinas should never, ever be without pockets."

There was a loud knock on the door.

"Uncle Leo! You're just in time for my
ballerina debut!" announced Emma.

She played her kazoo and banged two lids together. Now it sounded like burping with cymbals! That was much better than fancy flippy-fluttery music. And much louder.

Emma rolled like a tumbleweed.
Cartwheeled over the cat.
Tapped her toes.

When she finally ran out of breath, she sprawled on the floor.

Uncle Leo clapped. "You were wonderful, Emma! I never thought of you as a ballerina. I saw you more as the jungle explorer type. That's why I sent the safari outfit."

"What safari outfit?" she asked, showing him the box.

"They sent the wrong outfit!" he exclaimed.

Emma laughed. "Maybe I can be a ballerina *and* a jungle explorer, Uncle Leo."

She roared like a lion,

did a backward somersault,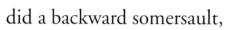

dipped into a curtsy, and
hollered, "Ta-da!"

And knocked over the fishbowl.

For Bob, Ben & Cory—
who love me even though I was born without a ballerina gene! —L.S.

For Sandrine and Arianne —A.W.

DIAL BOOKS FOR YOUNG READERS
A division of Penguin Young Readers Group
Published by The Penguin Group
Penguin Group (USA) Inc., 375 Hudson Street, New York, NY 10014, U.S.A.

Penguin Group (Canada), 90 Eglinton Avenue East, Suite 700, Toronto, Ontario, Canada M4P 2Y3 (a division of Pearson Penguin Canada Inc.) • Penguin Books Ltd, 80 Strand, London WC2R 0RL, England • Penguin Ireland, 25 St. Stephen's Green, Dublin 2, Ireland (a division of Penguin Books Ltd) • Penguin Group (Australia), 250 Camberwell Road, Camberwell, Victoria 3124, Australia (a division of Pearson Australia Group Pty Ltd) • Penguin Books India Pvt Ltd, 11 Community Centre, Panchsheel Park, New Delhi - 110 017, India • Penguin Group (NZ), 67 Apollo Drive, Rosedale, North Shore 0632, New Zealand (a division of Pearson New Zealand Ltd) • Penguin Books (South Africa) (Pty) Ltd, 24 Sturdee Avenue, Rosebank, Johannesburg 2196, South Africa • Penguin Books Ltd, Registered Offices: 80 Strand, London WC2R 0RL, England

Design by Nancy R. Leo-Kelly
Text set in Adobe Garamond
Manufactured in China on acid-free paper
1 3 5 7 9 10 8 6 4 2

Library of Congress Cataloging-in-Publication Data
Skeers, Linda.
Tutus aren't my style / by Linda Skeers ; pictures by Anne Wilsdorf.
p   cm.
Summary: When she receives a ballerina costume from her uncle, Emma, who does not know how to
be a ballerina, gets a lot of advice from friends and family.
ISBN 978-0-8037-3212-4
[1. Ballet dancing—Fiction. 2. Individuality—Fiction.] I. Wilsdorf, Anne, ill. II. Title. III. Title: Tutus are not my style.
PZ7.S62585Tu 2010   [E]—dc22   2009009284

The art was created using watercolor and China ink on white paper.

31901047070414